a World
without
Crime
Elijah Salmon

WORKBOOK PRESS LLC
187 E Warm Springs Rd,
Suite B285, Las Vegas, NV 89119, USA

Website:        https://workbookpress.com/
Hotline:        1-888-818-4856
Email:          admin@workbookpress.com

Ordering Information:
Quantity sales. Special discounts are available on quantity purchases by corporations, associations, and others.
For details, contact the publisher at the address above.

Library of Congress Control Number:

ISBN-13:        978-1-952754-86-9 (Paperback Version)
                978-1-952754-87-6 (Digital Version)

REV. DATE: 09/19/2022

# A World without Crime

BY: Elijah Salmon

# Dedication Page

*This is a way of acknowledging those who have helped me along the way.*

*My deepest appreciation to….*

*All those who encouraged me and helped me in prayer, project, and financial support to bring this book to completion; to my mother.*

*I want to thank also my friends and relatives; this book would not be complete without you.*

*Most importantly, my gratitude to the Lord and Savior Jesus for His grace and companionship during this project and the Holy Spirit's faithful guidance through this assignment.*

# Introduction

My name is James Seno. I'm 16 years old, living with my sister Lexis Seno she is 15 years old and our childhood friends Shan and his sister Ashley Lawson. Shan is 17 and his sister is 16. We also live with my parents who are Damon and Lisa and they are head of the police force. As I get ready for school, I hear Shan and Ashley fighting over the bathroom because Shan is taking too long in the bathroom. My sister calls up to us saying the food is ready. As I open my room door, I see Ashley at the bathroom door with her skirt on and her shirt in her hand covering her top. We meet eyes and run into our rooms. My face feels hot. Then I hear a knock at my door. It's Lexis. I open the door and she asks if I'm okay because my face is bright red. I say it's nothing and rush down the stairs to the table and sit down. Shan messes with me saying you had a treat didn't you as he's laughing. Ashley comes down with Lexis and shoots a glare at Shan and he looks away whistling. Ashley looks at me with an embarrassed face as she sits down. Mom and dad ask if everything is ok with me and Ashley. Ashley says everything is fine and quickly turns away. Mom says ok and brings the food to the table as she sits down and says eat quick you guys have to get ready to go to school. After we finish eating, we head off to school Lexis and Shan are ahead of me and Ashley. We see that Shan is trying to act cool as he joking around with Lexis. As we catch up, we hear Shan ask Lexis if she has a crush. Me and Ashley stop with shock emotion on our face. He tries to play it off by saying he wanted to know because the other guys in classes want to know. She looks at him with an embarrassed look on her face and asks how about you. Then Shan looks at me and Ashley asking us if we have crushes. I look at Shan saying (as I stutter) you know who I like. As I glance over at Ashley and she says there is no boy at the school that meets my standard. Shan looks at me and says to Ashley that's rough to say. She says well it's true, not knowing my feelings. Then I quickly say to Lexis and Shan just get together already everyone now you guys are crazy about each other. They both just stare at each other. Lexis says big brother and I laugh and say it's true. Lexis says if I don't stop, she will tell Ashley the truth. I say, ok ok you win. Ashley looks at us puzzled and says what do you mean Lexi? Oh, look where already able to see the school already let's go as I run ahead to the school and wait for the others. As they catch up, we agree to meet in front of the school at the end of the day after our club meetings are over. Me and Shan are in the tennis club and Ashley and Lexis are in the basketball club. We all nod in agreement and head off to class. As I head to my class Shan runs up to me asking, do you really like my sister? I look around making sure that no one hears him and say as I look at him why are you saying that in public he says just answer. I say you know the answer to that he says ok. I ask him why he asks. He says if you help me, I'll help you and then the bell for first period rings and he says we'll talk later. As I'm in class my phone vibrates. It scares me. The teacher tells me to settle down and the class laughs as I apologize and sit down. The teacher turns to the board and continues. I take my phone out and look at my messages from Ashley. She asked why I had run off like that and what was the meaning behind what Lexi said. I text back saying that I just wanted to stretch my legs and Lex was messing around. She responds saying ok talk later. I look at the message feeling relieved then think of what Shan said and I think he didn't mean what I think he means does he. I waited impatiently for the bell to ring so I could run to Shan's class. As I get ready to put my head on my desk to think more about it the bell rings. I grab my bag and quickly run to Shan class, but when I reach Shan class he's not there. I ask some friends of his where he went to and they say to his sister class I take off as fast I can. As I reach Ashley class I see her, Shan and my sister and I say Shan don't Ashley looks at me with an embarrassed and surprised look on her face. I ask did he tell you she looks at me and runs away. I look at Shan and say wasn't you supposed to talk to me first and Lexi says you should be thankful he did it for you I say how about this Shan loves you and dream about you. Then I ran after Ashley without looking back. I think of where Ashley would go at a time like this as I'm running down the halls looking for her. I think of the roof. I start heading to the roof. I hear the bell ring as I'm heading to the roof. I reach the last flight of stairs and run up them as I bust through the door and see Ashley sitting by the reeling with her head on her knees. An she looks up with tears in her eyes and she start to wipe the tears away and say why didn't you tell me I said all those things this morning I look at her and say I wanted to but I didn't know how to do it and I was nervous because I didn't know how you felt she's stand and says you're not the only one that felt that way about their feelings. I've waited for you to tell me how you felt about me. I love you but why did you have my brother tell me and not you? I walk to her and hug as I say I'm sorry I should have told you. As I'm holding her, I say I love you and she looks at me and says idiot as she kisses me. We head back towards class and we both agree to only tell Lexi and Shan about us. Then we kiss one more time and go back to class. As I'm in class I daydream about Ashley as I'm daydreaming the teacher calls me without me noticing and yells my name James! I snap out of it and stand up quickly and say yes. The teacher says stop daydreaming in the class as the class starts to laugh and I smile as I sit down my phone vibrates and I have a message from Lexi and Shan saying you jerk why would tell him that and Shan says I'm sorry I did that but that's was uncool. What I did and he had to chase after Lex and calm her down but they got together after they talked and said how they felt about each other. I respond to both of them and say sorry and then tell them about me and Ash got together to make up for what I did Shan takes awhile to respond. My sister says really, I'm happy for you guys and then Shan respond say finally congrats bro. I say thanks then we all agree to meet after club as it was getting closer to lunch all I could think about was Ashley as I'm daydreaming about Ashley, I get poked an snapped out it I look over to see Ashley, Shan, and Lex saying come on it's time for lunch I was shock how quickly time went by then realized I was daydreaming the whole time an say ok. As we head to lunch Shan says everyone finally got together huh? I say what did you think would happen as I look at the girls as they're blushing. When we got to the cafeteria it was full with kids eating their lunch so we headed to the lunch line to get our food and headed to the roof to eat and talk about how long we hide our feelings about each other and how the world was getting more dangerous with crime. I say that if I had some way to stop the crime that was going on in the world, I would ask you guys to join me. They look at me and laugh saying of course we would join you, wouldn't need to ask. The bell rings and we head to our next math class together since we all have the same math class. We grab our treys and throw them away in the trash by the roof door. As we walk to class Shan and Lexi call to me to show me their holding hands as to say to me, and Ashley should do the same. I look embarrassedly and shake my head as they look over excited for me to do it. I take a gulp and hold Ashley's hand as she looks at me with a smile and says you took my hand like she was waiting for me to do that. When we reach class just before the bell we sit in our seats and I look out the window as it is time for the teacher to come in and say hello to everyone. As I am looking out the window I start to daydream and think of how I'm finally with the one I truly love. Ashley taps me on my shoulder from behind saying what's wrong. I say I say nothing, just that I was thinking of you and how I have dreamed of this day to come when I wouldn't need to hide my feelings. She says as her face is bright red and looks away saying I was hoping that to and that it would come true before we graduated as I get ready to respond an announcement comes on saying they need the captains for tennis and basketball team to come to their club rooms. Their advisors need them. We get up and head to our club rooms. Me and Shan go to the tennis club room and Lex and Ash go to the basketball club room. In the tennis club room, we talked about upcoming tournaments and who would be doing doubles and singles and the players that would be in the tournament with us because we didn't have enough players due to injuries. Since we needed more time to think about it, we had to put it on hold. By the time we were done it was the end of the day. So, we left to go meet the girls to head home. As we were walking to meet the girls, we walked past the common area outside. I saw a notebook I think someone had dropped it earlier in the day. I told Shan to hold on as I went to go and pick up the book. He yelled to me what is it? I said I want to bring this notebook to the office when I get closer to it. I see on the cover writing saying taker of lives. I walk back to him and say never mind we'll talk when we get home. After words we headed towards the girls. As we came into view. The girls ran up to us and gave us hugs. Then we held hands with the girls and started walking as we talked about how classes were and what was going on with our clubs. As we got home, I asked everyone to come to my room and told them I had something to show them and they said ok when everyone came to my room. I took out the notebook and showed it to everyone. Ashley asks what the deal with the notebook is. I say I don't know on the way to meet you two with Shan. I notice it on the ground in the common area. Then Shan says he said he was going to take it to the office then changed his mind when he got closer to it. On the way to you girls. I say, hmmmm, when I saw the cover for some reason, I got curious. Lexis asks what's important about that notebook. I ask everyone to come over here as they got closer, they could see a name on the notebook taker of lives. Once everyone got close enough, I turned open the cover of the book inside of the cover there were rules saying how to use it. Explaining the rules saying you can write down a person or persons name in the book. You have to write the circumstance in 4minutes and 45 seconds or the notebook would not take effect. If you don't know the name or face of the person or persons they will not be affected by this notebook. The last rule says you can share this power with the people you want to share it with by having them kissing your hand or lip. We looked at each other as if we thought it, was a joke. But then again on the roof we talked about how we would stop crime if we had a way to but Lex and Ash said killing people is wrong and scary. Shan says it's up to you James we will agree with what you decide the girls nodded. I say we should see if we can really do what it says in this notebook. We turn the tv on and see that a bank is being robbed by 4 people whose name and face show up when they say who they are. Zack Ackson, Willie Nelson, AJ Carson and Sofia Willson, as I write their name down just their name, we watch the clock for 1:25

seconds to see if they die. I ask what if they really do die. Ashley says we will form a pact with you so we can change the world together Shan, and Lex agreed. I smiled as I said thanks to everyone for being with me. Shan says we will always have your back no matter what. We looked at the clock and it reached 1:25 second and we looked at the TV, the robbers were leaving the bank. So, we thought nothing was going to happen but when they were heading to the car, they all dropped to the ground. We looked at the tv as if it wasn't true. As we were all in shock, the phone rang and it was mom calling as she was with dad saying they weren't going to be home on time because something came up. Lex ask what came up. They said we can't say much but 4 suspects died and they had to stay to see how. Lex says ok and hangs up. We asked her what they said and she said mom and dad won't be home on time because of what happened on tv. That's when we all knew the book was real and it could grant the way to change the world. Ashley says to me make the pact with me so that way I can share the burden with you. That way you don't have to handle the burden alone and the others follow. I asked everyone if they were sure Shan said remember what I said on the roof you wouldn't need to ask us. If you have the power to do it. I just smiled and said, ``Let's change the world everyone". Ashley says I'm first and asks what we need to do. It says in the book all we need to do is have you say that you will not betray me and I will follow you anywhere and kiss me on the lips or hand. Ashley says the following words for the pact to be performed. I will not betray you and follow you anywhere and kiss me on the lips. She says I will allow this once you can kiss your sister on the lips, we both said idiot and laughed. Lexis went next saying I will not betray you and I will follow you anywhere big brother and kiss my hand. Shan says looks like I'm up and says remember where all here for you so don't think you alone man. Then he also says the words I will not betray you and will follow you anywhere and kiss my hand. Then we agreed that I should keep the book and Shan writes down the names of the people, Ashley keeps track of the police action and Lex monitors the websites for any criminals. We also came up with the idea that allows us to leave the notebook at home. We each get a sheet of paper out of the notebook. So, when we do our judgment, it would be at random times. It's been 2 weeks since we started doing this and we noticed that the world was heading in the right direction. As we were in my room watching the news and web for criminals' name. I had notice a shadow out of the corner of my eye. When I looked up it was a monster there, I screamed and everyone turned around asking what's wrong. I pointed at the shadow when they turned to look at it, it seemed as if they were frozen with fear. The monster says there's no reason to be scared seeing that all of you can see me mean you guys share the power knowing that's not an average notebook. The monster says my name is Han, a god of the underworld. That used to be my book of taker of lives and ask who's the one that picked up the notebook. I stand and say I am the one that picked it up. He says when that book is picked up by a human, we gods of the underworld become attached to that human and the people he made the pact with. We are able to leave when the book becomes complete or destroyed. If we don't want the book, we have to pass it on and have our memories erased of ever having it. The price of having the book is that we will experience the feeling only to those in Valhalla and also the torment of having the feeling of burning for eternity and that when you are reincarnated you will still feel these effects. When I heard that I was scared for everyone else when I was going to answer they grabbed me and hugged me saying James we are here for you didn't we make a pack. That's when Ashley kissed me and said don't worry okay, we're here for you as if they read my mind. Han asked if we made up our mind. I answered and said yes, we will keep it. He smiled and said that the notebook is now yours. It has been 1 week since then we all decided to be committed to this there was no turning back. The world had come to know us as the silent ones. Han had asked if that was about us. We said yes, the world had known there was someone judging the wicked he said really. Shan had said yes and gave an example saying if you were to have a survey asking if criminals would be punished by the law in most cases most would say no being that others know the law isn't always fair. So, most people wouldn't voice their opinion publicly on how criminals should be punished but online where you can be unknown. Our support is growing but in social circles where you can be judged by others, others would rather deny our existence because they are scared of what others will say. My phone rings and it's a message from mom saying we will be home later tonight. Something came up when I get ready to show everyone else a tv interruption come on saying their news from Georgia state police department. With news a man and woman appear on tv saying his name I am the detective known as Blake T

Watson otherwise known as T. Then the lady says I'm the other head detective Destiny R Carson otherwise known as R and that there's been murders going on throughout the world being done by the silent ones. And that we have set up our headquarters in Georgia and we plan to catch the masterminds involved. Han says this is interesting they are pretty sure they will catch you guys. I say with what evidence to back their claim to arrest us. Plus, they would need this notebook so otherwise it would be impossible. I say that being that we are trying to change the world of course the world law enforcement would try to resist so the police would have to get involved. Then the man on tv says that silent ones I have a pretty good idea of why you are doing this. So, you can be a god but to us you are evil Ashley gets up and says you think James is doing this to be god and that he is evil. He started doing this for the world not once did he think of becoming god. He is a good-natured person. If you think he's evil you will be eliminated Shan and Lex agreed with her. Ashley grabbed a pencil off the dresser and took out the piece of paper she had and wrote their name down. After she wrote down the detective's name, I looked at her as if she made a mistake because we were not supposed to be killing innocent people. Before I can panic something appears on tv and it is the letters representing the two detectives T and R. Saying we can't believe what just happened, silent ones you can kill without being physically involved or present. We wouldn't have believed it if we didn't just see this with ourselves. You see, we had to make sure that when you had killed them you if you had to be present or if you could from a distance. So, listen those two you just saw die weren't us being that they are dead now I should say where inmates that were sentenced for death today. it seems that you don't have access to these criminals. The lady says these criminals are not known to the world so you could not have heard about them. Now will you try to kill us again? Come on do it do it you scared come on ahh in a laughing manner so it looks like you can't do it can you? You have left us with something very interesting. There's also one more thing you don't know. This was said to be by the Georgia state police department but this is USPA and it's being aired in Georgia. The man says well to be more precise the reason we choose here first is because the first of your kills was only aired in Georgia but to be more sufficient in the henry county area. Then later on did you start judging all around the world but started to only focus on the United states. We look around at each other. The detective known as T continues by saying that we shouldn't just give up and hand ourselves in so that the way we kill will be found out and we will be sentenced to death and cut off. We stood there in a daze as I started to realize how real this got. I started to get excited and say do they believe we will just sit idly just to get caught. We will make the world a better place. If I have to be the god of this world then I will or should I say we will if you guys are still willing to stand by me. Shan says do you really need to ask or are you just saying that you want us by your side. I look at them as Ashley and Lex as they are smiling at me and I realize that we are all in this and ask them to stay by my side and they all answer yes. All of sudden Ashley comes to me and gives me a kiss and says I will never leave you. Han says humans are so interesting they each have to find each other not knowing each face. I say Lex call mom or dad to see how they are doing and see if they are coming home, she says ok. Shan and Ashley ask me what should they do as I'm about to answer Hon calls out to me, I say to them keep monitoring criminals and writing their name and I go to see what Hon's want I say yes you call for me he says do you know what makes god of death be able to kill humans besides our notebooks I say what. He says our ability to see the human lifespan. We don't need to know their face, just their name and their time of death and the number of years out of their lives we can receive. But the real prize is when we do, we can grant the user and the people he made a pact with our power but not only them but their offspring. I say that would make things a lot easier for the future situations and problems less stressful and my children and their offspring can continue our work but at what cost. He smiles and says half of yours and the others remaining life span for your offspring. I would also take half of their life span but if they do not have a pact within 3 months when they take the reins it will be their life. I say you want my children's life in return he says or I can take yours and give this to one of your friends but later on their grand kids will be stuck in the same situation. So, in all you will take one of our lives or kids or grands live in order for us to use this and our later generation will be in the same situation as us to use this power. He crackles and says yes so what will it be before I can answer I hear the gang say Hon how dare you try and force his hand like that. I look around to notice the others by my side and Ashley says James do not even consider this deal if you dare sacrifice your life, I will never forgive you and die with you I turn and grab her saying think of the possibilities we could have and if we to let me pay with my life our and the other kids would have this power without any risk until they take over. I know putting them in situation isn't idea but with cost of my life they wouldn't need to worry about this until they take over. She says what if you die before we have kids, then what or if you die when our kids are young, they will not only be without a father but also a mother because I would be with you. Shan and Lexis say she's right; you know we all would follow after you when you die how would you feel knowing not just your kids but also your niece and nephew were without their parents. I look at them and when I'm about to say something. Ashley put her finger on my lips as she says that's the end of the discussion. This will only be an option when we have no choice and say we will all be losing half of our lifespans. You are not just going to sacrifice yourself. When it comes to our kids will just have to deal with the same choice when the time comes, I look around and sign saying you guys win. I turn to Hon and say well there's your answer for that I turn to lexis to ask what our parents said when Hon say well their one with less risk you guys might want to know and consider Ashley says what is it. He says I can give you guys the power to see the name and lifespan of your victims but you would have to split the power between you meaning one will see the name and the other sees the lifespan. So, say James can see the name but not the lifespan so we have Ashley see the lifespan meaning you both would give up an eye for this and the same apply to Lexis and Shan. We all say we want to make this trade. He smiles and says you only be able to see when you activate the ability so in other words you will be blinding your partner. Before we all agree you, guys know that he is saying that we will not be able to use this power apart otherwise one of us will be blind otherwise if we do, we will be blind and cause us to be in an accident being that we are not all ways together. And there will be time when we have to be apart. Ashley says don't you dare try that on us we going with this deal and that finale ok. I turn to look at her but she has that look on her face of where its sadness but also the look of where she telling me not to take this on by myself, I say I want to be to see the lifespan, Ashley smiles say I'll take the names then Shan goes with same as his sister and Lexis goes with same as me. Hon says so I take it as you all agree we go to the mirror in the corner of my and Shan room and look into it and one of our eyes is yellow. I say dad and mom got contacts. We can use you hid the color of eye's Shan goes to get them. Lexis says mom and dad won't be coming home today they have a meeting. I say Ashley do you think you can hack into police system and have us see what's going on in the meeting. She says better I can hack their computer camera and have us be able to see and hear that way we can know what is going on and not be traced but if they look into it, they will notice it but not trace it back to us I say great get on it. That's when Shan comes back and I say ok everyone put them on Imma put my on in a minute I have a plan. I want me an Shan reading names and lifespan and lexis to right them but Shan as you are doing that I'm going to have you write name of people that lifespan that aren't supposed to die for a few months then have you write their name as precautions and to see if their due time change to that time we plan for them and then the ones that aren't due yet will be use after Ashley get us eye and ears in the meeting has we are putting the plan in action Ashley says I got us in but it seems to be at the end. Lisa says now for the most important part before ending how we identify who this individual is or group is if we can't find a pattern. A voice from a computer with a white screen with the letter R says the time may be random but look at the screen. They turn to a screen with a schedule with days and times on it. Some parts of day are black some are white and when they combine the days and time that are black you can see a pattern. Damon says on Monday through Friday a lot of the killings happen from 6am to 4pm and the weekend it happens later at 11am but goes on till 4pm and picks up again at 6pm till 12 am. T says so it tells us that it's a group of highschool students. Lisa, you think a bunch of highschoolers could do this. S says how early does school usually start for high schoolers. One of the detectives say unless they have school activities it usually starts at 8:30am and ends at 3:30pm for clubs like sports usually varies between those time during the school day they have practice 2 hrs. before school and sometime after. T says that's right plus the way they do their judgment leads us to individuals that have a very immature way of justice and aspire to become gods like. S says for now let go with this and look into schools in the henry districts and say anything else. Lisa says ok so if no one has anything else to say, the meeting adjourned and the camera we're connected to shuts off. I say ok this is the plan were going to keep the same pattern but write judgments for times we can't during class for tomorrow. Then the next day we have it to where there's judgments are every hour so they won't catch on that we heard there meeting. That way they aren't going to notice the change out right and notice that we have connection to the police. We only want T and S to notice but mom and dad might too but that's unavoidable. For the last part where we are going to change the days to every other day just when I finish the plan, I hear someone coming up the stairs. The other nod Shan hid the notebook behind the mirror on the makeshift shelf we made. We turn the tv on and me and Ashley sit on the floor in front of the bed Lexi and Shan sit on the bed and we hold hands and that's when the door opens and mom pops her head in and says, there you guys are when ya didn't answer we worried did you guys eat yet. I say no we were waiting for our parents to come home where starving she smiles and says you guys could have ordered. Shan says it wouldn't be the same without you and dad she says aww an about to leave an says don't think I didn't notice ya are hold hand finally romance has bloomed into flowers. Lexis says mom embarrassedly, mom says I know what I'm about to ask is a little weird but would you four mind sharing a room we'll put a curtain dividing the room into boys and girls with bunk beds because we have your cousins coming over in a few days. We look at each other and the girls blush and say if the boys don't mind, I say I'm good with it you Shan?  He says if your cool with it then so am I mom says guys are such good kids and says come down to eat closing the door. Ashley says s..so where going to be sleeping in the same room when I fully grasp the conversation fully that just happened, I say y…yea I guess so looking away and Shan and Lexis just sit there exchanging embarrassed looks. I go back to what T and S said about the times they didn't notice Henry county and Clayton county times are different by an hr. Shan says that right, I say so until they notice that our edge we get up and go down stairs for dinner.

********* END **********

9 781952 754869